The Abbey Grange

A New Sherlock Holmes Mystery

The Abbey Grange
A Sherlock Holmes Adventure

By: Arthur Conan Doyle

Series Editor: Craig Stephen Copland

The characters of Sherlock Holmes and Dr. Watson are in the public domain, as is the original story, The Abbey Grange.

Published by:

Conservative Growth
1101 30th Street NW. Ste. 500
Washington, DC, 20007

.

ISBN: 1537426664

ISBN-13: 978-1537426662

Dedication

Dame Jean Conan Doyle

This series of books, *The Stories of Sherlock Holmes in Large Print*, is appropriately dedicated to the memory of Jean Conan Doyle, the youngest daughter of Arthur Conan Doyle.

In addition to her years of service to the literary estate of her father and to the promotion of all things Sherlockian, Jean Conan Doyle was a highly accomplished woman in her own right. As a young woman she joined the Women's Auxiliary Air Force and served with distinction during World War II and afterward. She rose through the ranks until she was awarded the rank of Air Commandant in 1963. She was given the honor of OBE and appointed as honorary aide-de-camp to Queen Elizabeth II. Also in 1963, she was elevated to Dame Commander of the Order of the British Empire (DBE, Military Division), and became known as Dame Jean Conan Doyle.

This very impressive woman suffered from poor eyesight since she was a child and took an active interest in the welfare of the blind and those who were visually impaired. Upon her death, she donated the remaining copyrights she owned to the Royal National Institute for the Blind.

This new printing of the Canon of Sherlock Holmes stories in large print has been undertaken so that those with poor or diminishing eyesight can continue to enjoy reading and re-reading the adventures of their beloved detective. It is following in the footsteps of Dame Jean Conan Doyle not only in its service to the visually impaired, but also in its dedication to the continuing fascination with the character of Sherlock Holmes.

Acknowledgments

All books in this series of Sherlock Holmes mysteries use the font, APHont, that was developed specifically for texts for the visually impaired by the American Printing House for the Blind. The formatting also follows the recommendations provided by this organization. If you wish to volunteer or donate to them, they can be found at www.aph.org.

Spelling and punctuation follow British practices, as did the original story.

No edition of the stories of Sherlock Holmes could ever exist were it not for the original creative brilliance of the author, Arthur Conan Doyle. To his genius in creating the character of the world's favourite detective, all Sherlockians are forever grateful.

Thanks must also go to Jon Lellenberg who for many years served as counsel to the Arthur Conan Doyle Literary Estate and who generously provided advice and direction for this series of books.

In preparing the Editor's Notes that accompany every story, I am indebted to many sources for my far-from-scholarly knowledge of The Canon. I would, however, refer readers who wish to know more about Sherlock Holmes to the following excellent works:

Christopher Redmond, *The Sherlock Holmes Handbook.*

Leslie Klinger, *The New Annotated Sherlock Holmes,*

William S. Baring Gould, *The Annotated Sherlock Holmes,* and

D. Martin Dakin, *A Sherlock Holmes Commentary*.

If you notice any errors or omissions, or you have suggestions that would make these books even better for seniors and visually impaired readers, please report them to sherlock75holmes@aol.com.

The Abbey Grange

It was on a bitterly cold and frosty morning during the winter of '97 that I was awakened by a tugging at my shoulder. It was Holmes. The candle in his hand shone upon his eager, stooping face and told me at a glance that something was amiss.

"Come, Watson, come!" he cried. "The game is afoot. Not a word! Into your clothes and come!"

Ten minutes later we were both in a cab and rattling through the silent streets on our way to

Charing Cross Station. The first faint winter's dawn was beginning to appear, and we could dimly see the occasional figure of an early workman as he passed us, blurred and indistinct in the opalescent London reek. Holmes nestled in silence into his heavy coat, and I was glad to do the same, for the air was most bitter and neither of us had broken our fast. It was not until we had consumed some hot tea at the station, and taken our places in the Kentish train, that we were sufficiently thawed, he to speak and I to listen. Holmes drew a note from his pocket and read it aloud:—

   "Abbey Grange, Marsham, Kent,
      "3.30 a.m.

"MY DEAR MR. HOLMES,—I should be very glad of your immediate assistance in what promises to be a most remarkable case. It is something quite in your line. Except for releasing the lady I will see that everything is kept exactly as I have found it, but I beg you not to lose an instant, as it is difficult to leave Sir Eustace there.

"Yours faithfully, STANLEY HOPKINS."

"Hopkins has called me in seven times, and on each occasion his summons has been entirely justified," said Holmes. "I fancy that every one of his cases has found its way into your collection, and I must admit, Watson, that you have some power of selection which atones for much which I deplore in your narratives. Your fatal habit of looking at everything from the point of view of a story instead of as a scientific exercise has ruined what might have been an instructive and even classical series of demonstrations. You slur over work of the utmost finesse and delicacy in order to dwell upon sensational details which may excite, but cannot possibly instruct, the reader."

"Why do you not write them yourself?" I said, with some bitterness.

"I will, my dear Watson, I will. At present I am, as you know, fairly busy, but I propose to devote my declining years to the composition of a text-book which shall focus the whole art of detection into one volume. Our present research appears to be a case of murder."

"You think this Sir Eustace is dead, then?"

"I should say so. Hopkins's writing shows considerable agitation, and he is not an emotional man. Yes, I gather there has been violence, and that the body is left for our inspection. A mere suicide would not have caused him to send for me. As to the release of the lady, it would appear that she has been locked in her room during the tragedy. We are moving in high life, Watson; crackling paper, 'E.B.' monogram, coat-of-arms, picturesque address. I think that friend Hopkins will live up to his reputation and that we shall have an interesting morning. The crime was committed before twelve last night."

"How can you possibly tell?"

"By an inspection of the trains and by reckoning the time. The local police had to be called in, they had to communicate with Scotland Yard, Hopkins had to go out, and he in turn had to send for me. All that makes a fair night's work. Well, here we are at Chislehurst Station, and we shall soon set our doubts at rest."

A drive of a couple of miles through narrow country lanes brought us to a park gate, which was opened for us by an old lodge-keeper, whose haggard face bore the reflection of some great disaster. The avenue ran through a noble park, between lines of ancient elms, and ended in a low, widespread house, pillared in front after the fashion of Palladio. The central part was evidently of a great age and shrouded in ivy, but the large windows showed that modern changes had been carried out, and one wing of the house appeared to be entirely new. The youthful figure and alert, eager face of Inspector Stanley Hopkins confronted us in the open doorway.

"I'm very glad you have come, Mr. Holmes. And you too, Dr. Watson! But, indeed, if I had my time over again I should not have troubled you, for since the lady has come to herself she has given so clear an account of the affair that there is not much left for us to do. You remember that Lewisham gang of burglars?"

"What, the three Randalls?"

"Exactly; the father and two sons. It's their work. I have not a doubt of it. They did a job at Sydenham a fortnight ago, and were seen and described. Rather cool to do another so soon and so near, but it is they, beyond all doubt. It's a hanging matter this time."

"Sir Eustace is dead, then?"

"Yes; his head was knocked in with his own poker."

"Sir Eustace Brackenstall, the driver tells me."

"Exactly—one of the richest men in Kent. Lady Brackenstall is in the morning-room. Poor lady, she has had a most dreadful experience. She seemed half dead when I saw her first. I think you had best see her and hear her account of the facts. Then we will examine the dining-room together."

Lady Brackenstall was no ordinary person. Seldom have I seen so graceful a figure, so womanly a presence, and so beautiful a face. She was a blonde, golden-haired, blue-eyed, and would, no doubt, have had the perfect complexion which goes with such colouring had not her recent experience left her drawn and haggard. Her sufferings were physical as well as mental, for over one eye rose a hideous, plum-coloured swelling, which her maid, a tall, austere woman, was bathing assiduously with vinegar and water. The lady lay back exhausted upon a couch, but her quick, observant gaze as we entered the room, and the alert expression of her beautiful features, showed that neither her wits nor her courage had been shaken by her terrible experience. She was enveloped in a loose dressing-gown of blue and silver, but a black sequin-covered dinner-dress was hung upon the couch beside her.

"I have told you all that happened, Mr. Hopkins," she said, wearily; "could you not repeat it for me? Well, if you think it necessary, I will tell these gentlemen what occurred. Have they been in the dining-room yet?"

"I thought they had better hear your ladyship's story first."

"I shall be glad when you can arrange matters. It is horrible to me to think of him still lying there." She shuddered and buried her face in her hands. As she did so the loose gown fell back from her forearms. Holmes uttered an exclamation.

"You have other injuries, madam! What is this?" Two vivid red spots stood out on one of the white, round limbs. She hastily covered it.

"It is nothing. It has no connection with the hideous business of last night. If you and your friend will sit down I will tell you all I can.

"I am the wife of Sir Eustace Brackenstall. I have been married about a year. I suppose that it is no use my attempting to conceal that our marriage has not been a happy one. I fear that all our neighbours would tell you that, even if I were to attempt to deny it. Perhaps the fault may be partly mine. I was brought up in the freer, less conventional atmosphere of South Australia, and this English life, with its proprieties and its primness, is not congenial to me. But the main reason lies in the one fact which is notorious to everyone, and that is that Sir Eustace was a confirmed drunkard. To be with such a man for an hour is unpleasant. Can you imagine what it means for a sensitive and high-spirited woman to be tied to him for day and night? It is a sacrilege, a crime, a villainy to hold that such a marriage is binding. I say that these monstrous laws of yours will bring a curse upon the land—Heaven will not let such wickedness endure." For an instant she sat up, her cheeks flushed, and her eyes blazing from under the terrible mark upon her brow. Then the strong, soothing hand of the austere maid drew her head down on to the cushion, and the wild anger died away into passionate sobbing. At last she continued:—

"I will tell you about last night. You are aware, perhaps, that in this house all servants sleep in the modern wing. This central block is made up of the dwelling-rooms, with the kitchen behind and our bedroom above. My maid Theresa sleeps above my room. There is no one else, and no sound could alarm those who are in the farther wing. This must have been well known to the robbers, or they would not have acted as they did.

"Sir Eustace retired about half-past ten. The servants had already gone to their quarters. Only my maid was up, and she had remained in her room at the top of the house until I needed her services. I sat until after eleven in this room, absorbed in a book. Then I walked round to see that all was right before I went upstairs. It was my custom to do this myself, for, as I have explained, Sir Eustace was not always to be trusted. I went into the kitchen, the butler's pantry, the gun-room, the billiard-room, the drawing-room, and finally the dining-room. As I approached the window, which is covered with thick curtains, I suddenly felt the wind blow upon my face and realized that it was open. I flung the curtain aside and found myself face to face with a broad-shouldered, elderly man who had just stepped into the room. The window is a long French one, which really forms a door leading to the lawn. I held my bedroom candle lit in my hand, and, by its light, behind the first man I saw two others, who were in the act of entering. I stepped back, but the fellow was on me in an instant. He caught me first by the wrist and then by the throat. I opened my mouth to scream, but he struck me a savage blow with his fist over the eye, and felled me to the ground. I must have been unconscious for a few minutes, for when I came to myself I found that they had torn down the bell-rope and had secured me tightly to the oaken chair which stands at the head of the dining-room table. I was so firmly bound that I could not move, and a handkerchief round my mouth prevented me from uttering any sound. It was at this instant that my unfortunate husband entered the room. He had evidently heard some suspicious sounds, and he came prepared for such a scene as he found. He was dressed in his shirt and trousers, with his favourite blackthorn cudgel in his hand. He rushed at one of the burglars, but another—it was the elderly man—stooped, picked the poker out of the grate, and struck him a horrible blow as he passed. He fell without a groan, and never moved again. I fainted once more, but again it could only have been a very few minutes during which I was insensible. When I opened my eyes I found that they had collected the silver from the sideboard, and they had drawn a bottle of wine which stood there. Each of them had a glass in his hand. I have already told you, have I not, that one was elderly, with a beard, and the others young, hairless lads. They might have been a father with his two sons. They

14

talked together in whispers. Then they came over and made sure that I was still securely bound. Finally they withdrew, closing the window after them. It was quite a quarter of an hour before I got my mouth free. When I did so my screams brought the maid to my assistance. The other servants were soon alarmed, and we sent for the local police, who instantly communicated with London. That is really all that I can tell you, gentlemen, and I trust that it will not be necessary for me to go over so painful a story again."

"Any questions, Mr. Holmes?" asked Hopkins.

"I will not impose any further tax upon Lady Brackenstall's patience and time," said Holmes. "Before I go into the dining-room I should like to hear your experience." He looked at the maid.

"I saw the men before ever they came into the

house," said she. "As I sat by my bedroom window I saw three men in the moonlight down by the lodge gate yonder, but I thought nothing of it at the time. It was more than an hour after that I heard my mistress scream, and down I ran, to find her, poor lamb, just as she says, and him on the floor with his blood and brains over the room. It was enough to drive a woman out of her wits, tied there, and her very dress spotted with him; but she never wanted courage, did Miss Mary Fraser of Adelaide, and Lady Brackenstall of Abbey Grange hasn't learned new ways. You've questioned her long enough, you gentlemen, and now she is coming to her own room, just with her old Theresa, to get the rest that she badly needs."

With a motherly tenderness the gaunt woman put her arm round her mistress and led her from the room.

"She has been with her all her life," said Hopkins. "Nursed her as a baby, and came with her to England when they first left Australia eighteen months ago. Theresa Wright is her name, and the kind of maid you don't pick up nowadays. This way, Mr. Holmes, if you please!"

The keen interest had passed out of Holmes's expressive face, and I knew that with the mystery all the charm of the case had departed. There still remained an arrest to be effected, but what were these commonplace rogues that he should soil his hands with them? An abstruse and learned specialist who finds that he has been called in for a case of measles would experience something of the annoyance which I read in my friend's eyes. Yet the scene in the dining-room of the Abbey Grange was sufficiently strange to arrest his attention and to recall his waning interest.

It was a very large and high chamber, with carved oak ceiling, oaken panelling, and a fine array of deer's heads and ancient weapons around the walls. At the farther end from the door was the high French window of which we had heard. Three smaller windows on the right-hand side filled the apartment with cold winter sunshine. On the left was a large, deep fireplace, with a massive, over-hanging oak mantelpiece. Beside the fireplace was a heavy oaken chair with arms and cross-bars at the bottom. In and out through the open woodwork was woven a crimson cord, which was secured at each side to the crosspiece below. In releasing the lady the cord had been slipped off her, but the knots with which it had been secured still remained. These details only struck our attention afterwards, for our thoughts were entirely absorbed by the terrible object which lay upon the tiger-skin hearthrug in front of the fire.

It was the body of a tall, well-made man, about forty years of age. He lay upon his back, his face upturned, with his white teeth grinning through his short black beard. His two clenched hands were raised above his head, and a heavy blackthorn stick lay across them. His dark, handsome, aquiline features were convulsed into a spasm of vindictive hatred, which had set his dead face in a terribly fiendish expression. He had evidently been in his bed when the alarm had broken out, for he wore a foppish embroidered night-shirt, and his bare feet projected from his trousers. His head was horribly injured, and the whole room bore witness to the savage ferocity of the blow which had struck him down. Beside him lay the heavy poker, bent into a curve by the concussion. Holmes examined both it and the indescribable wreck which it had wrought.

"He must be a powerful man, this elder Randall," he remarked.

"Yes," said Hopkins. "I have some record of the fellow, and he is a rough customer."

"You should have no difficulty in getting him."

"Not the slightest. We have been on the look-out for him, and there was some idea that he had got away to America. Now that we know the gang are here I don't see how they can escape. We have the news at every seaport already, and a reward will be offered before evening. What beats me is how they could have done so mad a thing, knowing that the lady could describe them, and that we could not fail to recognise the description."

"Exactly. One would have expected that they would have silenced Lady Brackenstall as well."

"They may not have realized," I suggested, "that she had recovered from her faint."

"That is likely enough. If she seemed to be senseless they would not take her life. What about this poor fellow, Hopkins? I seem to have heard some queer stories about him."

"He was a good-hearted man when he was sober, but a perfect fiend when he was drunk, or rather when he was half drunk, for he seldom really went the whole way. The devil seemed to be in him at such times, and he was capable of anything. From what I hear, in spite of all his wealth and his title, he very nearly came our way once or twice. There was a scandal about his drenching a dog with petroleum and setting it on fire—her ladyship's dog, to make the matter worse— and that was only hushed up with difficulty. Then he threw a decanter at that maid, Theresa Wright; there was trouble about that. On the whole, and between ourselves, it will be a brighter house without him. What are you looking at now?"

Holmes was down on his knees examining with great attention the knots upon the red cord with which the lady had been secured. Then he carefully scrutinized the broken and frayed end where it had snapped off when the burglar had dragged it down.

"When this was pulled down the bell in the

kitchen must have rung loudly," he remarked.

"No one could hear it. The kitchen stands right at the back of the house."

"How did the burglar know no one would hear it? How dared he pull at a bell-rope in that reckless fashion?"

"Exactly, Mr. Holmes, exactly. You put the very question which I have asked myself again and again. There can be no doubt that this fellow must have known the house and its habits. He must have perfectly understood that the servants would all be in bed at that comparatively early hour, and that no one could possibly hear a bell ring in the kitchen. Therefore he must have been in close league with one of the servants. Surely that is evident. But there are eight servants, and all of good character."

"Other things being equal," said Holmes, "one would suspect the one at whose head the master threw a decanter. And yet that would involve treachery towards the mistress to whom this woman seems devoted. Well, well, the point is a minor one, and when you have Randall you will probably find no difficulty in securing his accomplice. The lady's story certainly seems to be corroborated, if it needed corroboration, by every detail which we see before us." He walked to the French window and threw it open. "There are no signs here, but the ground is iron hard, and one would not expect them. I see that these candles on the mantelpiece have been lighted."

"Yes; it was by their light and that of the lady's bedroom candle that the burglars saw their way about."

"And what did they take?"

"Well, they did not take much—only half-a-dozen articles of plate off the sideboard. Lady Brackenstall thinks that they were themselves so disturbed by the death of Sir Eustace that they did not ransack the house as they would otherwise have done."

"No doubt that is true. And yet they drank some wine, I understand."

"To steady their own nerves."

"Exactly. These three glasses upon the sideboard have been untouched, I suppose?"

"Yes; and the bottle stands as they left it."

"Let us look at it. Halloa! Halloa! What is this?"

The three glasses were grouped together, all of them tinged with wine, and one of them containing some dregs of bees-wing. The bottle stood near them, two-thirds full, and beside it lay a long, deeply-stained cork. Its appearance and the dust upon the bottle showed that it was no common vintage which the murderers had enjoyed.

A change had come over Holmes's manner. He had lost his listless expression, and again I saw an alert light of interest in his keen, deep-set eyes. He raised the cork and examined it minutely.

"How did they draw it?" he asked.

Hopkins pointed to a half-opened drawer. In it lay some table linen and a large cork-screw.

"Did Lady Brackenstall say that screw was used?"

"No; you remember that she was senseless at the moment when the bottle was opened."

"Quite so. As a matter of fact that screw was NOT used. This bottle was opened by a pocket-screw, probably contained in a knife, and not more than an inch and a half long. If you examine the top of the cork you will observe that the screw was driven in three times before the cork was extracted. It has never been transfixed. This long screw would have transfixed it and drawn it with a single pull. When you catch this fellow you will find that he has one of these multiplex knives in his possession."

an abbey cathedral

"Excellent!" said Hopkins.

"But these glasses do puzzle me, I confess. Lady Brackenstall actually SAW the three men drinking, did she not?"

"Yes; she was clear about that."

"Then there is an end of it. What more is to be said? And yet you must admit that the three glasses are very remarkable, Hopkins. What, you see nothing remarkable! Well, well, let it pass. Perhaps when a man has special knowledge and special powers like my own it rather encourages him to seek a complex explanation when a simpler one is at hand. Of course, it must be a mere chance about the glasses. Well, good morning, Hopkins. I don't see that I can be of any use to you, and you appear to have your case very clear. You will let me know when Randall is arrested, and any further developments which may occur. I trust that I shall soon have to congratulate you upon a successful conclusion. Come, Watson, I fancy that we may employ ourselves more profitably at home."

During our return journey I could see by Holmes's face that he was much puzzled by something which he had observed. Every now and then, by an effort, he would throw off the impression and talk as if the matter were clear, but then his doubts would settle down upon him again, and his knitted brows and abstracted eyes would show that his thoughts had gone back once more to the great dining-room of the Abbey Grange in which this midnight tragedy had been enacted. At last, by a sudden impulse, just as our train was crawling out of a suburban station, he sprang on to the platform and pulled me out after him.

"Excuse me, my dear fellow," said he, as we watched the rear carriages of our train disappearing round a curve; "I am sorry to make you the victim of what may seem a mere whim, but on my life, Watson, I simply CAN'T leave that case in this condition. Every instinct that I possess cries out against it. It's wrong—it's all wrong—I'll swear that it's wrong. And yet the lady's story was complete, the maid's corroboration was sufficient, the detail was fairly exact. What have I to put against that? Three wine-glasses, that is all. But if I had not taken things for granted, if I had examined everything with care which I would have shown had we approached the case DE NOVO and had no cut-and-dried story to warp my mind, would I not then have found something more definite to go upon? Of course I should. Sit down on this bench, Watson, until a train for Chislehurst arrives, and allow me to lay the evidence before you, imploring you in the first instance to dismiss from your mind the idea that anything which the maid or her mistress may have said must necessarily be true. The lady's charming personality must not be permitted to warp our judgment.

"Surely there are details in her story which, if we looked at it in cold blood, would excite our suspicion. These burglars made a considerable haul at Sydenham a fortnight ago. Some account of them and of their appearance was in the papers, and would naturally occur to anyone who wished to invent a story in which imaginary robbers should play a part. As a matter of fact, burglars who have done a good stroke of business are, as a rule, only too glad to enjoy the proceeds in peace and quiet without embarking on another perilous undertaking. Again, it is unusual for burglars to operate at so early an hour; it is unusual for burglars to strike a lady to prevent her screaming, since one would imagine that was the sure way to make her scream; it is unusual for them to commit murder when their numbers are sufficient to overpower one man; it is unusual for them to be content with a limited plunder when there is much more within their reach; and finally I should say that it was very unusual for such men to leave a bottle half empty. How do all these unusuals strike you, Watson?"

"Their cumulative effect is certainly considerable, and yet each of them is quite possible in itself. The most unusual thing of all, as it seems to me, is that the lady should be tied to the chair."

"Well, I am not so clear about that, Watson; for it is evident that they must either kill her or else secure her in such a way that she could not give immediate notice of their escape. But at any rate I have shown, have I not, that there is a certain element of improbability about the lady's story? And now on the top of this comes the incident of the wine-glasses."

"What about the wine-glasses?"

"Can you see them in your mind's eye?"

"I see them clearly."

"We are told that three men drank from them. Does that strike you as likely?"

"Why not? There was wine in each glass."

"Exactly; but there was bees-wing only in one glass. You must have noticed that fact. What does that suggest to your mind?"

"The last glass filled would be most likely to contain bees-wing."

"Not at all. The bottle was full of it, and it is inconceivable that the first two glasses were clear and the third heavily charged with it. There are two possible explanations, and only two. One is that after the second glass was filled the bottle was violently agitated, and so the third glass received the bees-wing. That does not appear probable. No, no; I am sure that I am right."

"What, then, do you suppose?"

"That only two glasses were used, and that the dregs of both were poured into a third glass, so as to give the false impression that three people had been here. In that way all the bees-wing would be in the last glass, would it not? Yes, I am convinced that this is so. But if I have hit upon the true explanation of this one small phenomenon, then in an instant the case rises from the commonplace to the exceedingly remarkable, for it can only mean that Lady Brackenstall and her maid have deliberately lied to us, that not one word of their story is to be believed, that they have some very strong reason for covering the real criminal, and that we must construct our case for ourselves without any help from them. That is the mission which now lies before us, and here, Watson, is the Chislehurst train."

The household of the Abbey Grange were much surprised at our return, but Sherlock Holmes, finding that Stanley Hopkins had gone off to report to head-quarters, took possession of the dining-room, locked the door upon the inside, and devoted himself for two hours to one of those minute and laborious investigations which formed the solid basis on which his brilliant edifices of deduction were reared. Seated in a corner like an interested student who observes the demonstration of his professor, I followed every step of that remarkable research. The window, the curtains, the carpet, the chair, the rope—each in turn was minutely examined and duly pondered. The body of the unfortunate baronet had been removed, but all else remained as we had seen it in the morning. Then, to my astonishment, Holmes climbed up on to the massive mantelpiece. Far above his head hung the few inches of red cord which were still attached to the wire. For a long time he gazed upward at it, and then in an attempt to get nearer to it he rested his knee upon a wooden bracket on the wall. This brought his hand within a few inches of the broken end of the rope, but it was not this so much as the bracket itself which seemed to engage his attention. Finally he sprang down with an ejaculation of satisfaction.

"It's all right, Watson," said he. "We have got our case— one of the most remarkable in our collection. But, dear me, how slow-witted I have been, and how nearly I have committed the blunder of my lifetime! Now, I think that with a few missing links my chain is almost complete."

"You have got your men?"

"Man, Watson, man. Only one, but a very formidable person. Strong as a lion—witness the blow that bent that poker. Six foot three in height, active as a squirrel, dexterous with his fingers; finally, remarkably quick-witted, for this whole ingenious story is of his concoction. Yes, Watson, we have come upon the handiwork of a very remarkable individual. And yet in that bell-rope he has given us a clue which should not have left us a doubt."

"Where was the clue?"

"Well, if you were to pull down a bell-rope, Watson, where would you expect it to break? Surely at the spot where it is attached to the wire. Why should it break three inches from the top as this one has done?"

"Because it is frayed there?"

"Exactly. This end, which we can examine, is frayed. He was cunning enough to do that with his knife. But the other end is not frayed. You could not observe that from here, but if you were on the mantelpiece you would see that it is cut clean off without any mark of fraying whatever. You can reconstruct what occurred. The man needed the rope. He would not tear it down for fear of giving the alarm by ringing the bell. What did he do? He sprang up on the mantelpiece, could not quite reach it, put his knee on the bracket—you will see the impression in the dust— and so got his knife to bear upon the cord. I could not reach the place by at least three inches, from which I infer that he is at least three inches a bigger man than I. Look at that mark upon the seat of the oaken chair! What is it?"

"Blood."

"Undoubtedly it is blood. This alone puts the lady's story out of court. If she were seated on the chair when the crime was done, how comes that mark? No, no; she was placed in the chair AFTER the death of her husband. I'll wager that the black dress shows a corresponding mark to this. We have not yet met our Waterloo, Watson, but this is our Marengo, for it begins in defeat and ends in victory. I should like now to have a few words with the nurse Theresa. We must be wary for awhile, if we are to get the information which we want."

She was an interesting person, this stern Australian nurse. Taciturn, suspicious, ungracious, it took some time before Holmes's pleasant manner and frank acceptance of all that she said thawed her into a corresponding amiability. She did not attempt to conceal her hatred for her late employer.

"Yes, sir, it is true that he threw the decanter at

me. I heard him call my mistress a name, and I told him that he would not dare to speak so if her brother had been there. Then it was that he threw it at me. He might have thrown a dozen if he had but left my bonny bird alone. He was for ever illtreating her, and she too proud to complain. She will not even tell me all that he has done to her. She never told me of those marks on her arm that you saw this morning, but I know very well that they come from a stab with a hat-pin. The sly fiend—Heaven forgive me that I should speak of him so, now that he is dead, but a fiend he was if ever one walked the earth. He was all honey when first we met him, only eighteen months ago, and we both feel as if it were eighteen years. She had only just arrived in London. Yes, it was her first voyage—she had never been from home before. He won her with his title and his money and his false London ways. If she made a mistake she has paid for it, if ever a woman did. What month did we meet him? Well, I tell you it was just after we arrived. We arrived in June, and it was July. They were married in January of last year. Yes, she is down in the morning-room again, and I have no doubt she will see you, but you must not ask too much of her, for she has gone through all that flesh and blood will stand."

Lady Brackenstall was reclining on the same couch, but looked brighter than before. The maid had entered with us, and began once more to foment the bruise upon her mistress's brow.

"I hope," said the lady, "that you have not come to cross-examine me again?"

"No," Holmes answered, in his gentlest voice, "I will not cause you any unnecessary trouble, Lady Brackenstall, and my whole desire is to make things easy for you, for I am convinced that you are a much-tried woman. If you will treat me as a friend and trust me you may find that I will justify your trust."

"What do you want me to do?"

"To tell me the truth."

"Mr. Holmes!"

"No, no, Lady Brackenstall, it is no use. You may have heard of any little reputation which I possess. I will stake it all on the fact that your story is an absolute fabrication."

Mistress and maid were both staring at Holmes with pale faces and frightened eyes.

"You are an impudent fellow!" cried Theresa. "Do you mean to say that my mistress has told a lie?"

Holmes rose from his chair.

"Have you nothing to tell me?"

"I have told you everything."

"Think once more, Lady Brackenstall. Would it not be better to be frank?"

For an instant there was hesitation in her beautiful face. Then some new strong thought caused it to set like a mask.

"I have told you all I know."

Holmes took his hat and shrugged his shoulders. "I am sorry," he said, and without another word we left the room and the house. There was a pond in the park, and to this my friend led the way. It was frozen over, but a single hole was left for the convenience of a solitary swan. Holmes gazed at it and then passed on to the lodge gate. There he scribbled a short note for Stanley Hopkins and left it with the lodge-keeper.

"It may be a hit or it may be a miss, but we are bound to do something for friend Hopkins, just to justify this second visit," said he. "I will not quite take him into my confidence yet. I think our next scene of operations must be the shipping office of the Adelaide-Southampton line, which stands at the end of Pall Mall, if I remember right. There is a second line of steamers which connect South Australia with England, but we will draw the larger cover first."

Holmes's card sent in to the manager ensured instant attention, and he was not long in acquiring all the information which he needed. In June of '95 only one of their line had reached a home port. It was the ROCK OF GIBRALTAR, their largest and best boat. A reference to the passenger list showed that Miss Fraser of Adelaide, with her maid, had made the voyage in her. The boat was now on her way to Australia, somewhere to the south of the Suez Canal. Her officers were the same as in '95, with one exception. The first officer, Mr. Jack Croker, had been made a captain and was to take charge of their new ship, the BASS ROCK, sailing in two days' time from Southampton. He lived at Sydenham, but he was likely to be in that morning for instructions, if we cared to wait for him.

No; Mr. Holmes had no desire to see him, but would be glad to know more about his record and character.

His record was magnificent. There was not an officer in the fleet to touch him. As to his character, he was reliable on duty, but a wild, desperate fellow off the deck of his ship, hot-headed, excitable, but loyal, honest, and kind-hearted. That was the pith of the information with which Holmes left the office of the Adelaide-Southampton company. Thence he drove to Scotland Yard, but instead of entering he sat in his cab with his brows drawn down, lost in profound thought. Finally he drove round to the Charing Cross telegraph office, sent off a message, and then, at last, we made for Baker Street once more.

"No, I couldn't do it, Watson," said he, as we re-entered our room. "Once that warrant was made out nothing on earth would save him. Once or twice in my career I feel that I have done more real harm by my discovery of the criminal than ever he had done by his crime. I have learned caution now, and I had rather play tricks with the law of England than with my own conscience. Let us know a little more before we act."

Before evening we had a visit from Inspector Stanley Hopkins. Things were not going very well with him.

"I believe that you are a wizard, Mr. Holmes. I really do sometimes think that you have powers that are not human. Now, how on earth could you know that the stolen silver was at the bottom of that pond?"

"I didn't know it."

"But you told me to examine it."

"You got it, then?"

"Yes, I got it."

"I am very glad if I have helped you."

"But you haven't helped me. You have made the affair far more difficult. What sort of burglars are

47

they who steal silver and then throw it into the nearest pond?"

"It was certainly rather eccentric behaviour. I was merely going on the idea that if the silver had been taken by persons who did not want it, who merely took it for a blind as it were, then they would naturally be anxious to get rid of it."

"But why should such an idea cross your mind?"

"Well, I thought it was possible. When they came out through the French window there was the pond, with one tempting little hole in the ice, right in front of their noses. Could there be a better hiding-place?"

"Ah, a hiding-place—that is better!" cried Stanley Hopkins. "Yes, yes, I see it all now! It was early, there were folk upon the roads, they were afraid of being seen with the silver, so they sank it in the pond, intending to return for it when the coast was clear. Excellent, Mr. Holmes—that is better than your idea of a blind."

"Quite so; you have got an admirable theory. I have no doubt that my own ideas were quite wild, but you must admit that they have ended in discovering the silver."

"Yes, sir, yes. It was all your doing. But I have had a bad set-back."

"A set-back?"

"Yes, Mr. Holmes. The Randall gang were arrested in New York this morning."

"Dear me, Hopkins! That is certainly rather against your theory that they committed a murder in Kent last night."

"It is fatal, Mr. Holmes, absolutely fatal. Still, there are other gangs of three besides the

Randalls, or it may be some new gang of which the police have never heard."

"Quite so; it is perfectly possible. What, are you off?"

Yes, Mr. Holmes; there is no rest for me until I have got to the bottom of the business. I suppose you have no hint to give me?"

"I have given you one."

"Which?"

"Well, I suggested a blind."

"But why, Mr. Holmes, why?"

"Ah, that's the question, of course. But I commend the idea to your mind. You might possibly find that there was something in it. You won't stop for dinner? Well, good-bye, and let us know how you get on."

Dinner was over and the table cleared before Holmes alluded to the matter again. He had lit his pipe and held his slippered feet to the cheerful blaze of the fire. Suddenly he looked at his watch.

"I expect developments, Watson."

"When?"

"Now—within a few minutes. I dare say you thought I acted rather badly to Stanley Hopkins just now?"

"I trust your judgment."

"A very sensible reply, Watson. You must look at it this way: what I know is unofficial; what he knows is official. I have the right to private judgment, but he has none. He must disclose all, or he is a traitor to his service. In a doubtful case I would not put him in so painful a position, and so I reserve my information until my own mind is clear upon the matter."

"But when will that be?"

"The time has come. You will now be present at the last scene of a remarkable little drama."

There was a sound upon the stairs, and our door was opened to admit as fine a specimen of manhood as ever passed through it. He was a very tall young man, golden-moustached, blue-eyed, with a skin which had been burned by tropical suns, and a springy step which showed that the huge frame was as active as it was strong. He closed the door behind him, and then he stood with clenched hands and heaving breast, choking down some overmastering emotion.

"Sit down, Captain Croker. You got my telegram?"

Our visitor sank into an arm-chair and looked from one to the other of us with questioning eyes.

"I got your telegram, and I came at the hour you said. I heard that you had been down to the office. There was no getting away from you. Let's hear the worst. What are you going to do with me? Arrest me? Speak out, man! You can't sit there and play with me like a cat with a mouse."

"Give him a cigar," said Holmes. "Bite on that, Captain Croker, and don't let your nerves run away with you. I should not sit here smoking with you if I thought that you were a common criminal, you may be sure of that. Be frank with me, and we may do some good. Play tricks with me, and I'll crush you."

"What do you wish me to do?"

"To give me a true account of all that happened at the Abbey Grange last night—a TRUE account, mind you, with nothing added and nothing taken off. I know so much already that if you go one inch off the straight I'll blow this police whistle from my window and the affair goes out of my hands for ever."

The sailor thought for a little. Then he struck his leg with his great, sun-burned hand.

"I'll chance it," he cried. "I believe you are a man of your word, and a white man, and I'll tell you the whole story. But one thing I will say first. So far as I am concerned I regret nothing and I fear nothing, and I would do it all again and be proud of the job. Curse the beast, if he had as many lives as a cat he would owe them all to me! But it's the lady, Mary— Mary Fraser—for never will I call her by that accursed name. When I think of getting her into trouble, I who would give my life just to bring one smile to her dear face, it's that that turns my soul into water. And yet—and yet—what less could I do? I'll tell you my story, gentlemen, and then I'll ask you as man to man what less could I do.

"I must go back a bit. You seem to know everything, so I expect that you know that I met her when she was a passenger and I was first officer of the ROCK OF GIBRALTAR. From the first day I met her she was the only woman to me. Every day of that voyage I loved her more, and many a time since have I kneeled down in the darkness of the night watch and kissed the deck of that ship because I knew her dear feet had trod it. She was never engaged to me. She treated me as fairly as ever a woman treated a man. I have no complaint to make. It was all love on my side, and all good comradeship and friendship on hers. When we parted she was a free woman, but I could never again be a free man.

"Next time I came back from sea I heard of her marriage. Well, why shouldn't she marry whom she liked? Title and money— who could carry them better than she? She was born for all that is beautiful and dainty. I didn't grieve over her marriage. I was not such a selfish hound as that. I just rejoiced that good luck had come her way, and that she had not thrown herself away on a penniless sailor. That's how I loved Mary Fraser.

"Well, I never thought to see her again; but last voyage I was promoted, and the new boat was not yet launched, so I had to wait for a couple of months with my people at Sydenham. One day out in a country lane I met Theresa Wright, her old maid. She told me about her, about him, about everything. I tell you, gentlemen, it nearly drove me mad. This drunken hound, that he should dare to raise his hand to her whose boots he was not worthy to lick! I met Theresa again. Then I met Mary herself— and met her again. Then she would meet me no more. But the other day I had a notice that I was to start on my voyage within a week, and I determined that I would see her once before I left. Theresa was always my friend, for she loved Mary and hated this villain almost as much as I did. From her I learned the ways of the house. Mary used to sit up reading in her own little room downstairs. I crept round there last night and scratched at the window. At first she would not open to me, but in her heart I know that now she loves me, and she could not leave me in the frosty night. She whispered to me to come round to the big front window, and I found it open before me so as to let me into the dining-room. Again I heard from her own lips things that made my blood boil, and again I cursed this brute who mishandled the woman that I loved. Well, gentlemen, I was standing with her just inside the window, in all innocence, as Heaven is my judge, when he rushed like a madman into the room, called her the vilest name that a man could use to a woman, and welted her across the face with the stick he had in his hand. I had sprung for the poker, and it was a fair fight between us. See here on my arm where his first blow fell. Then it was my turn, and I went through him as if he had been a rotten pumpkin. Do you think I was sorry? Not I! It was his life or mine, but far more than that it was his life or hers, for how could I leave her in the power of this madman? That was how I killed him. Was I wrong? Well, then, what would either of you gentlemen have done if you had been in my position?

"She had screamed when he struck her, and that brought old Theresa down from the room above. There was a bottle of wine on the sideboard, and I opened it and poured a little between Mary's lips, for she was half dead with the shock. Then I took a drop myself. Theresa was as cool as ice, and it was her plot as much as mine. We must make it appear that burglars had done the thing. Theresa kept on repeating our story to her mistress, while I swarmed up and cut the rope of the bell. Then I lashed her in her chair, and frayed out the end of the rope to make it look natural, else they would wonder how in the world a burglar could have got up there to cut it. Then I gathered up a few plates and pots of silver, to carry out the idea of a robbery, and there I left them with orders to give the alarm when I had a quarter of an hour's start. I dropped the silver into the pond and made off for Sydenham, feeling that for once in my life I had done a real good night's work. And that's the truth and the whole truth, Mr. Holmes, if it costs me my neck."

Holmes smoked for some time in silence. Then he crossed the room and shook our visitor by the hand.

"That's what I think," said he. "I know that every word is true, for you have hardly said a word which I did not know. No one but an acrobat or a sailor could have got up to that bell-rope from the bracket, and no one but a sailor could have made the knots with which the cord was fastened to the chair. Only once had this lady been brought into contact with sailors, and that was on her voyage, and it was someone of her own class of life, since she was trying hard to shield him and so showing that she loved him. You see how easy it was for me to lay my hands upon you when once I had started upon the right trail."

"I thought the police never could have seen through our dodge."

"And the police haven't; nor will they, to the best of my belief. Now, look here, Captain Croker, this is a very serious matter, though I am willing to admit that you acted under the most extreme provocation to which any man could be subjected. I am not sure that in defense of your own life your action will not be pronounced legitimate. However, that is for a British jury to decide. Meanwhile I have so much sympathy for you that if you choose to disappear in the next twenty-four hours I will promise you that no one will hinder you."

"And then it will all come out?"

"Certainly it will come out."

The sailor flushed with anger.

"What sort of proposal is that to make a man? I know enough of law to understand that Mary would be had as accomplice. Do you think I would leave her alone to face the music while I slunk away? No, sir; let them do their worst upon me, but for Heaven's sake, Mr. Holmes, find some way of keeping my poor Mary out of the courts."

Holmes for a second time held out his hand to the sailor.

"I was only testing you, and you ring true every time. Well, it is a great responsibility that I take upon myself, but I have given Hopkins an excellent hint, and if he can't avail himself of it I can do no more. See here, Captain Croker, we'll do this in due form of law. You are the prisoner. Watson, you are a British jury, and I never met a man who was more eminently fitted to represent one. I am the judge. Now, gentleman of the jury, you have heard the evidence. Do you find the prisoner guilty or not guilty?"

"Not guilty, my lord," said I.

"Vox populi, vox Dei. You are acquitted, Captain Croker. So long as the law does not find some other victim you are safe from me. Come back to this lady in a year, and may her future and yours justify us in the judgment which we have pronounced this night."

About the Author

Arthur Conan Doyle

Arthur Conan Doyle was born on May 22, 1859, in Edinburgh, Scotland, the second of Charles and Mary Doyle's seven children. His mother, a well-educated woman and gifted storyteller, introduced her son to the traditions of chivalry, knights and their quests, and the joys of imaginative narratives. His father, however, struggled with alcoholism and mental illness and, as a result, the family was far from wealthy.

At the age of nine, Doyle was sent to a Jesuit boarding school in England where he remained for several years. Upon graduation he entered the University of Edinburgh Medical School and during his time there also studied botany at the Royal Botanic Garden in Edinburgh. While studying, Doyle began writing short stories. During a medical externship in Birmingham, he wrote his first published piece, "The Mystery of Sasassa Valley," a story set in South Africa. It was printed in *Chambers's Edinburgh Journal* on September 6, 1879.

While in medical school, he met the exceptional man who became his mentor, Professor Dr. Joseph Bell, whose brilliant powers of observation followed by logical deduction Doyle later credited as the inspiration for Sherlock Holmes.

His first gainful employment as a doctor was as a medical officer on the steamship *Mayumba* as it travelled to the West African Coast. After that job, he set up a medical practice first in Plymouth, and then in Southsea, near Portsmouth. Over the next few years, he worked both as a doctor and a writer. In 1885, Doyle met and married his first wife, Louisa Hawkins. They moved to Montague Place near the British Museum and not far from Baker Street. They had a daughter and a son, Mary and Kingsley, but in 1893, Louisa contracted tuberculosis and suffered from it far many years.

In the spring of 1886, Doyle wrote a mystery novel, *A Tangled Skein*. He was not initially successful in getting it published, but in November of that year, with the name changed to *A Study in Scarlet,* it was accepted for publication in the 1887 *Beeton's Christmas Annual*. *A Study in Scarlet*, which introduced Sherlock Holmes and Dr. Watson, was not immediately popular. His second short novel, *The*

Sign of the Four, likewise met with limited popularity. Beginning in the summer of 1891 his tales about the adventures of Sherlock Holmes began to appear in *The Strand Magazine* and then his popularity and that of Sherlock Holmes and Dr. Watson started to grow quickly in both Great Britain and the United States. Over the new four decades, Doyle would write sixty stories about Sherlock Holmes.

Having achieved fame and financial success as a writer, Doyle, at the age of thirty-two, quit medicine and devoted his time to writing. Throughout the later years of the nineteenth century and the first two decades of the twentieth, he wrote many other novels, short stories, histories, and essays. His most famous historical novel, *The White Company,* was published in 1891. Other fiction included a novel about the Napoleonic Era called *The Great Shadow,* published in 1892, and, in 1896, *Rodney*

Stone, a story connected to the sport of boxing. His two-volume account of the Boer War, praising the British armed forces, led to his being knighted.

Although he wished to be recognized for his more serious literary writings, Doyle became and remains famous primarily for his stories about Sherlock Holmes. From the 1890s on he would write his most popular Sherlock Holmes books, including, *The Adventures of Sherlock Holmes* (1892), *The Memoirs of Sherlock Holmes*(1894) and *The Hound of the Baskervilles* (1901). All of these stories and most of his other short stories and essays originally appeared in *The Strand* magazine and were subsequently published in other magazines in the United States, and in book form as anthologies.

By 1893, Doyle wanted to rid himself of Sherlock Holmes so that he could concentrate his efforts on his other literary pursuits, especially writing more historical fiction. He killed off Holmes in the story *The Final Problem,* in which Holmes and the arch-villain Professor Moriarty fall to their death in the gorge of Reichenbach Falls in Switzerland.

The fans of Sherlock Holmes/Arthur Conan Doyle were disappointed and readership of *The Strand* plummeted. In 1901, Doyle reintroduced Sherlock Holmes in *The Hound of the Baskervilles,* setting the date of the story before Holmes's death. A few years later, after the period known to Sherlockians as *The Great Hiatus,* Doyle brought Sherlock Holmes back to life in *The Adventure of the Empty House.* He did so not in response to pressure from the reading public and his publishers, but primarily as a result of a exceptionally generous offer from the American magazine, *Collier's Weekly*.

In 1906, his wife Louisa finally succumbed to tuberculosis. The following year, he married again, this time to his longtime friend, Jean Leckie. They had three children – Denis, Adrian, and Jean - and they remained married until Doyle died.

During the final years of his life, Doyle travelled extensively on lecture tours to North America, Europe and the Antipodes, promoting Spiritualism. He continued to write about his religious convictions in a series of books, including *The New Revelation* (1918), *The Vital Message*(1919), *The Wanderings of a Spiritualist* (1921) and *History of Spiritualism*(1926).

In 1928, Doyle's final twelve stories about Sherlock Holmes were published in a compilation entitled *The Case-Book of Sherlock Holmes*.

He continued his interest in and promotion of Spiritualism until his death, at age 71, in 1930.

While some of his other writings, such as *The White Company,* and the *Professor Challenger* stories— especially the first in the series, *The Lost World*— continue to be enjoyed to this day by dedicated Sherlockians, Arthur Conan Doyle's undisputed gift to hundreds of millions of readers over the past century has been the stories and the character of Sherlock Holmes, the world's most famous detective.

Editor's Notes

By Craig Stephen Copland, Editor, and author of *The New Sherlock Holmes Mysteries.*

(www.SherlockHolmesMystery.com)

Abbey Grange was published in September 1904 in *The Strand* and in *Collier's* at the end of December of the same year. Opinion as to its rank in the Canon is divided among Sherlockians. Some see it as one of the finest, and others as merely middling.

Although not unique to this story by any means, the central issue of the narrative is Holmes's decision, yet again, to take the law into his own hands and let a trio of people who participated in the killing of a man lie to the police and evade prosecution. And he does this because he considers them innocent, and acts in obedience to his conscience, not the law.

Holmes's actions are the basis for vigorous debate amongst Sherlockian scholars. He was, after all, invited into the case by Inspector Hopkins, not by Lady Brackenby. Scotland Yard is the client and will presumably pay a fee for Holmes's time. Holmes gives the earnest inspector a few clues, and then allows him to be misled whilst the real killers go free. He appears to believe that Mary Frazer, her maid, and Jack Croker acted in self-defense and would not be convicted. But he takes it upon himself, with Watson as mock jury, to pronounce upon their innocence. Even those of us who are devoted Sherlockians have to raise an eyebrow on this one.

I had long associated the phrase "vox populi, vox dei" with left-leaning governments, claiming a convenient recasting of the divine right of kings. It goes back a long way, however, and has been used to support the legitimacy of elections by universal (or nearly so) suffrage, and the use of trials by jury. It is in this latter sense that Holmes invokes it in this story.

Linked to the issue of justice, however, are the "monstrous laws" of England regarding divorce and property rights. Leslie Klinger brings to our attention that Arthur Conan Doyle was personally involved in attempts to have England's divorce laws reformed. As it was, they were terribly biased towards the husband, and even a wife who was regularly beaten could not claim a divorce without the combination of persistence maltreatment and adultery. Mary Frazer/Lady Brackenby, in this case, was horribly stuck.

The story does have some examples of brilliant

detection and deduction. The standard methods of detection had, by this time, generally started with a re-enactment of the crime. Where were the victims at the time? What were they doing? How did the villain enter? What did he do? What weapon was used? And so on. And does the evidence support or contradict the account of the witnesses?

Holmes is the master of this process and the incident of the wine glasses is one of the most brilliant of his observations and deductions. The reader is not denied access to the clue, but we lack his oenophile's knowledge to understand it. Other clues lead him to the sailor, the sailor to the shipping company, and the shipping company to Jack Croker—all within a matter of hours.

Some of the more incidental elements of the story are also of interest.

It is the only story in which the unjustifiably famous words of "Come, Watson. The game is afoot" are actually uttered. He never uses those words anywhere else. Who knew?

There are some nice literary touches to the story. The long, rambling introduction by Watson, and the chatter back and forth between him and Holmes is completely absent. Watson is awakened on a cold morning and the game is afoot.

The sentences ...

The first faint winter's dawn was beginning to appear, and we could dimly see the occasional figure of an early workman as he passed us, blurred and indistinct in the opalescent London reek. Holmes nestled in silence into his heavy coat, and I was glad to do the same, for the air was most bitter, and neither of us had broken our fast.

... are lyrically, poetically descriptive. Doyle is indulging his literary skills and we welcome them.

Doyle/Watson appears to have a soft spot in his heart for plucky, beautiful young women who are making their own way in the world. He also admires the gung-ho, unvarnished attitude of the Australians. Combine the two, and the victim/heroine is irresistible.

So, what do you think? Was Holmes right? Or did he cross one line too many?

About the Series Editor

Elementary, my dear reader. What else, after fifty years of enjoying the stories of Sherlock Holmes, is a recently retired gentleman to do with his time but write more stories about the world's most beloved detective.

Craig Stephen Copland confesses that he discovered Sherlock Holmes when, some time in the muddled early 1960s he pinched his older brother's copy of the immortal stories and was forever afterward thoroughly hooked. He is very grateful to his high school English teachers in Toronto who inculcated in him a love of literature and writing, and even inspired him to be an English major at the University of Toronto. There he was blessed to sit at the feet of both Northrup Frye and Marshall McLuhan, and other great literary professors, who led him to believe that he was called to be a high school English teacher.

It was his good fortune to come to his pecuniary senses and abandoned that goal and pursued a varied professional career that took him to over one hundred countries and endless adventures. He considers himself to have been and to continue to be one of the luckiest men on God's good earth.

A few years back he took a step in the direction of Sherlockian studies and joined the Sherlock Holmes Society of Canada—also known as the

Toronto Bootmakers. In May of 2014 this esteemed group of scholars announced a contest for the writing of a new Sherlock Holmes mystery. Although he had never tried his hand at fiction before, Craig entered and was pleasantly surprised to be selected as one of the winners. Having enjoyed the experience he decided to write more of the same, and is now on a mission to write a new Sherlock Holmes mystery that is related to and inspired by each of the sixty stories in the original Canon.

If you are interested in reading yet more Sherlock Holmes pastiche mysteries, you should checkout Craig's website:

www.SherlockHolmesMystery.com

All of the stories are set in Victorian/Edwardian London – with a few trips to other locations – and revolve around the traditional characters of Holmes and Watson, as well as the characters in the original story. But then a whole new mystery is unveiled. The New Sherlock Holmes Mysteries are available in large print, and fonts and formats designed for those who are visually impaired. They are available from online sources in most countries:

For personal and family reasons Craig became concerned about the lack of a Large Print format of the Canon that made use of the latest best practices in special fonts and recommended colors and layouts for the visually impaired and the elderly. As a result he undertook to re-published all of the Sherlock Holmes stories in this new Large Print series.

He currently lives and writes in Toronto, New York, the Okanagan Valley, and Tokyo, and looks forward to finally settling down when he turns ninety.

Have you read all sixty of the original stories and need more Sherlock Holmes?

The editor of *Sherlock Holmes in Large Print,* Craig Stephen Copland, writes Sherlock Holmes pastiche mysteries. He is a new Sherlock Holmes mystery as a tribute to each of the sixty original stories.

All are available in LARGE PRINT at SherlockHolmesMystery.com and all contain a copy of the original Sherlock Holmes story that inspired the new mystery.

The ones shown here are now published. The rest are on their way.

A NEW SHERLOCK HOLMES MYSTERY

STUDYING SCARLET

CRAIG STEPHEN COPLAND

A NEW SHERLOCK HOLMES MYSTERY

THE SIGN OF THE THIRD

CRAIG STEPHEN COPLAND

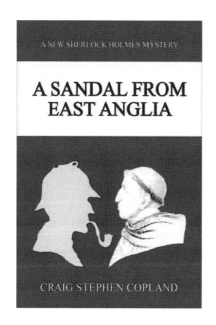

A NEW SHERLOCK HOLMES MYSTERY

A SANDAL FROM EAST ANGLIA

CRAIG STEPHEN COPLAND

A New Sherlock Holmes Mystery

The Bald-Headed Trust

Craig Stephen Copland

A NEW SHERLOCK HOLMES MYSTERY

A CASE OF
IDENTITY THEFT

CRAIG STEPHEN COPLAND

A NEW SHERLOCK HOLMES STORY

THE
HUDSON VALLEY
MYSTERY

CRAIG STEPHEN COPLAND

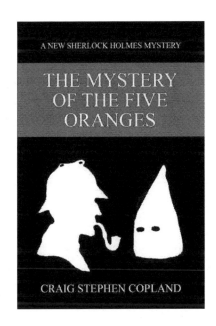

A NEW SHERLOCK HOLMES MYSTERY

THE MYSTERY
OF THE FIVE
ORANGES

CRAIG STEPHEN COPLAND

A NEW SHERLOCK HOLMES MYSTERY

THE MAN WHO
WAS TWISTED
BUT HIP

CRAIG STEPHEN COPLAND

A NEW SHERLOCK HOLMES MYSTERY

THE ADVENTURE
OF THE BLUE
BELT BUCKLE

CRAIG STEPHEN COPLAND

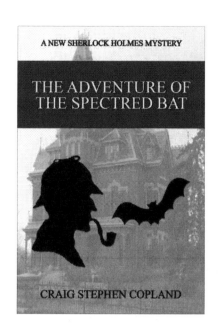

A NEW SHERLOCK HOLMES MYSTERY

THE ADVENTURE OF
THE SPECTRED BAT

CRAIG STEPHEN COPLAND

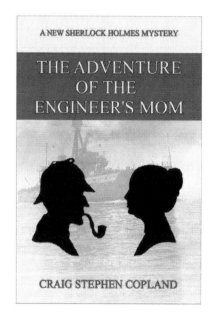

A NEW SHERLOCK HOLMES MYSTERY

THE ADVENTURE
OF THE
ENGINEER'S MOM

CRAIG STEPHEN COPLAND

A NEW SHERLOCK HOLMES MYSTERY

THE ADVENTURE OF
THE NOTABLE
BACHELORETTE

CRAIG STEPHEN COPLAND

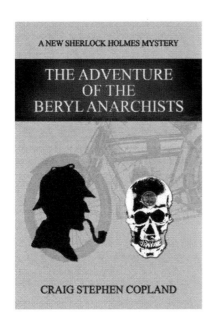

A NEW SHERLOCK HOLMES MYSTERY

THE ADVENTURE
OF THE
BERYL ANARCHISTS

CRAIG STEPHEN COPLAND

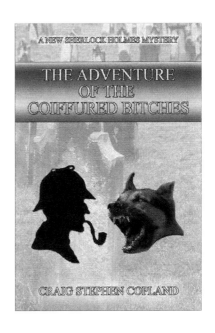

A NEW SHERLOCK HOLMES MYSTERY

THE ADVENTURE
OF THE
COIFFURED BITCHES

CRAIG STEPHEN COPLAND

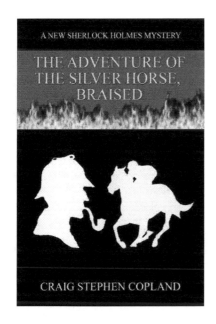

A NEW SHERLOCK HOLMES MYSTERY

THE ADVENTURE OF
THE SILVER HORSE,
BRAISED

CRAIG STEPHEN COPLAND

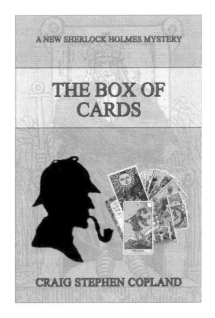

A NEW SHERLOCK HOLMES MYSTERY

THE BOX OF
CARDS

CRAIG STEPHEN COPLAND

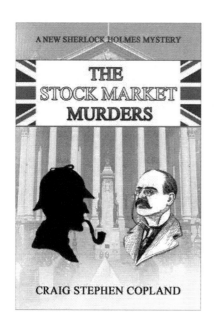

A NEW SHERLOCK HOLMES MYSTERY

THE
STOCK MARKET
MURDERS

CRAIG STEPHEN COPLAND

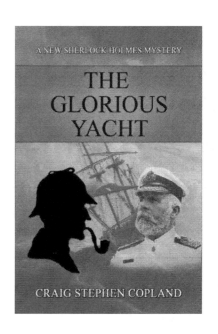

A NEW SHERLOCK HOLMES MYSTERY

THE
GLORIOUS
YACHT

CRAIG STEPHEN COPLAND

A NEW SHERLOCK HOLMES MYSTERY

A MOST GRAVE
RITUAL

CRAIG STEPHEN COPLAND

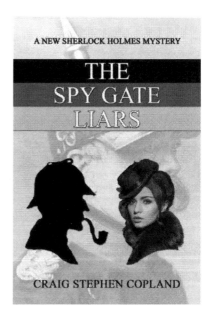

A NEW SHERLOCK HOLMES MYSTERY

THE
SPY GATE
LIARS

CRAIG STEPHEN COPLAND

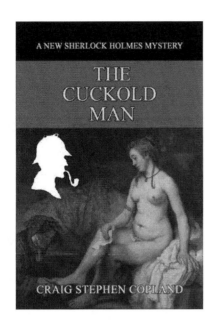

A NEW SHERLOCK HOLMES MYSTERY

THE CUCKOLD MAN

CRAIG STEPHEN COPLAND

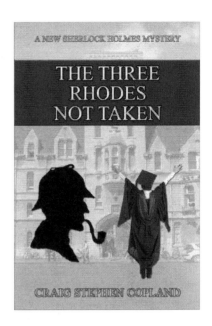

A NEW SHERLOCK HOLMES MYSTERY

THE THREE RHODES NOT TAKEN

CRAIG STEPHEN COPLAND

AN ESSAY IN THE GREAT GAME

SHERLOCK AND BARACK

How the *Sherlock Holmes Factor* Decided the Election of November 2012

CRAIG STEPHEN COPLAND

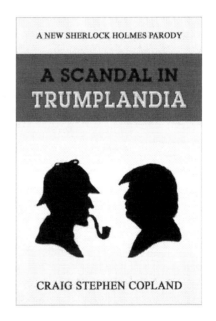

A NEW SHERLOCK HOLMES PARODY

A SCANDAL IN TRUMPLANDIA

CRAIG STEPHEN COPLAND

Made in the USA
Lexington, KY
08 April 2018